This book belongs to:

· ·

For Jemima, Ruben, Finn and Michael – my inspirations G.D.

For Sabrina A.B.

First published 2014 by order of the Tate Trustees by Tate Publishing,
a division of Tate Enterprises Ltd, Millbank, London SW1P 4RG
www.tate.org.uk/publishing

Text © Gabby Dawnay 2014. Illustrations © Alex Barrow 2014
A catalogue record for this book is available from the British Library
ISBN 978-1-84976-221-2

Distributed in the United States and Canada by ABRAMS, New York
Library of Congress Control Number applied for
Colour reproduction by Evergreen Colour Management Ltd. Hong Kong
Printed in China by Toppan Leefung Printing Ltd

A POSSUM'S TAIL

Gabby Dawnay & Alex Barrow

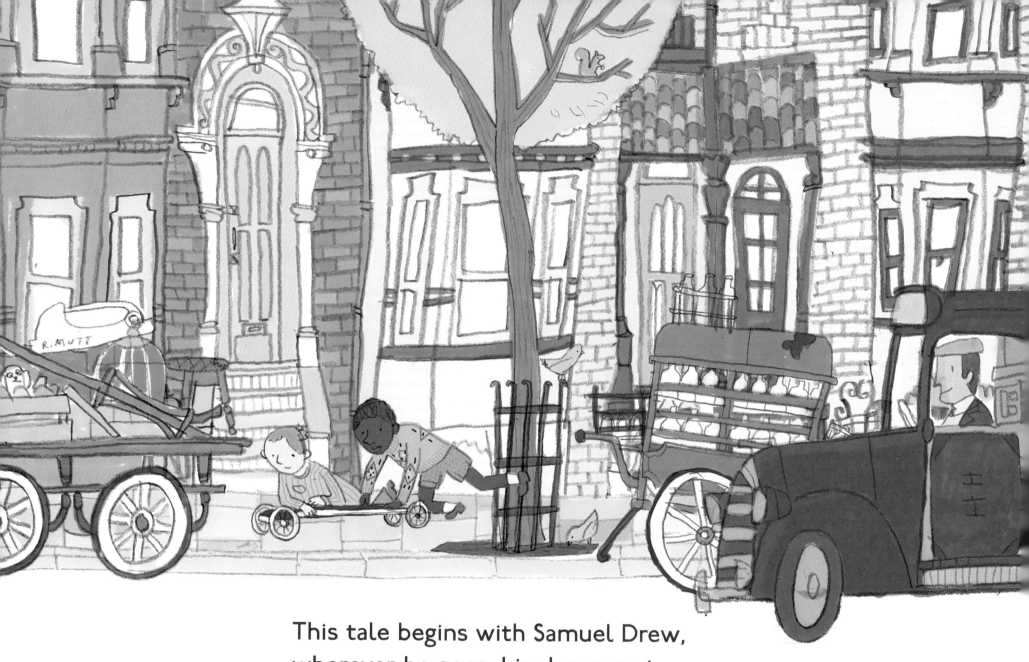

This tale begins with Samuel Drew,
wherever he goes, his dog goes too.
The day is fine, the sky is bright,
as Sam and dog stroll into sight.

Look there he is, the little boy
with dog-on-wheels, his favourite toy.
Let's watch and find out where they go...
But hurry up – we can't be slow!

They pass the pub and cross the street,
the dog on wheels, the boy on feet.

Past people walking up and down
the busy streets of London Town.

They pass the man who sells balloons,
they pass the band that's playing tunes.

They pass the market, pass the stand
that's selling news to all the land.

They pass the guards all standing straight,
they pass the tourists by the gate.

With cameras clicking, shopping dropping,
Sam and dog are still not stopping...

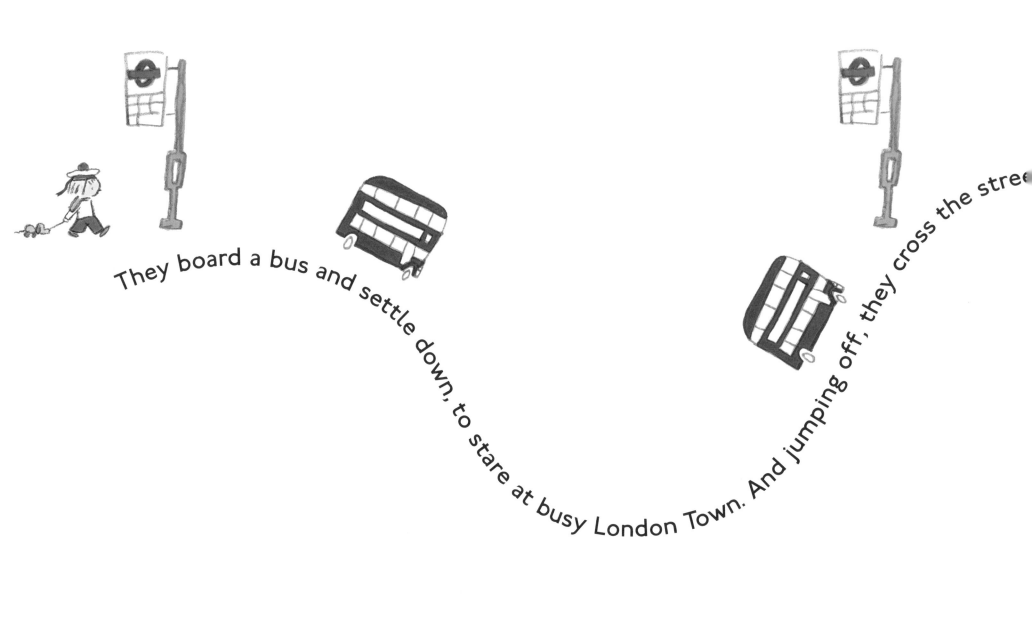

They board a bus and settle down, to stare at busy London Town. And jumping off, they cross the stree e dog on wheels, the boy on feet. What are those gates? Why, Samuel Drew, it seems you've come to...

...London Zoo!

They pass the cheeky chimpanzees and noisy parrots in the trees. Past hippos snoozing in the sun and sliding penguins having fu

...st sleeping snakes and tigers snoring, tall giraffes and lions roaring... Sam looks around, he knows his mind, he knows exactly where to find...

...the fluffy POSSUM fa-mi-ly,
it's them he really wants to see.
Five possums hanging upside down
in London Zoo, in London Town.

Sam watches, waits, his dog waits too.
What will the possums start to do?
They're all asleep. No games today!
But when Sam starts to walk away...

...the possums race to join the trail and hold on tight to doggy's tail!

Hey Sam, you'd better look behind – you'll be surprised at what you find!

Back past giraffes and lions growling, sleeping snakes and tigers prowling. They pass the penguins one by or

...d hippos snoozing in the sun. Back past the parrots in the trees, still squawking at the chimpanzees.

Back past the guards, still standing straight,
back past the tourists by the gate.

With cameras clicking, flashing, popping.
Whoops! Watch out for all that shopping!

Back through the market, past the stand,
still selling news to all the land.

Back past the band still playing tunes,
back past the man who sells balloons.

Back past the pub across the street,
the dog on wheels, the boy on feet.

At last they're home, it's time for tea.
When Sam turns round what does he see?
His dog...

...plus possums: one, two, three,
and four and five. They're hungry, too!
You'd better feed them, Samuel Drew.

The furry fellows sit and wait
for Sam to fill each empty plate
with sandwiches and cakes and... string?!
Not string! Their favourite thing on which to cling!

The wind picks up and off they go,
the possums floating in a row.
'Come back!' shouts Sam, as up they fly,
across the sunny London sky.

Sam watches as they drift away,
so sorry that they didn't stay...
'But my, that flying does look fun',
thinks Sam, and follows at a run!

What are those gates? It can't be true!
The possums bob above the...

...ZOO!

And here it is the possums drop.
Then back inside their pen they hop,
safe home to mum, and can you see?
They're just in time to have their tea!

THE END